BIOGRAPHIES

MATTHEW HENSON

by A.M. Reynolds

PEBBLE
a capstone imprint

Pebble Explore is published by Pebble, an imprint of Capstone.
1710 Roe Crest Drive
North Mankato, Minnesota 56003
www.capstonepub.com

Library of Congress Cataloging-in-Publication Data is available on the Library of Congress website.
ISBN: 978-1-9771-2332-9 (hardcover)
ISBN: 978-1-9771-2657-3 (paperback)
ISBN: 978-1-9771-2340-4 (eBook PDF)

Summary: How much do you know about Matthew Henson? Find out the facts you need to know about this explorer of the Arctic. You'll learn about the early life, challenges, and major accomplishments of this important American.

Image Credits
Alamy: Chronicle, 15; Getty Images: Hulton Archive/Keystone, 25, UIG/bildagentur-online, 13; Granger: 18; Library of Congress: 5, 7, 11, 16, 17, 29; Newscom: akg-images, 14, Everett Collection, 21; North Wind Picture Archives, 6, 8, 23; Science Source: Photo Researchers, Inc., cover, 1; Shutterstock: Curly Pat (geometric background), cover, back cover, 2, 29, IgorGolovniov, 26; Wikimedia: U.S. Navy/Chief Mass Communication Specialist Bill Mesta, 27

Editorial Credits
Editor: Anna Butzer; Designer: Elyse White; Media Researcher: Svetlana Zhurkin; Production Specialist: Spencer Rosio

Printed in the United States
PO117

Table of Contents

Words in **bold** are in the glossary.

Who Was Matthew Henson?

Matthew Henson was a brave African American explorer. He traveled the world. He was one of the first people to reach the North Pole. This area is the most northern point of Earth. It is very icy and cold there. It took eight tries to get there, but Matthew never gave up.

Matthew Henson in 1910

Growing Up Matthew

Matthew Henson was born more than 150 years ago on August 8, 1866. His parents were poor black **sharecroppers** in Maryland. Matthew grew up with three sisters.

Sharecroppers working outside their cabin

U.S. Capitol, Washington, D.C.

Matthew's mother died when he was 4 years old. The family moved to Washington, D.C., to find work. His father died when Matthew was only 9. Matthew and his sisters were **orphans**. They lived with relatives in Washington, D.C.

A harbor in Baltimore, Maryland

Matthew ran away when he was 11. He wanted to go on adventures. He asked a ship's captain for a job. Captain Childs was a very kind man. He hired Matthew as a cabin boy.

The captain taught Matthew how to read and write. He also taught him how to use maps and steer the ship. They sailed to many places, such as China, Japan, and Africa. Matthew was interested in how people in other places lived. He liked to learn new languages.

Matthew Keeps Trying

Matthew was happy living at sea. But Captain Childs died in 1884. Matthew left the ship. He worked as a store clerk in Washington, D.C. The store he worked at bought and sold animal furs.

One day in 1887, Matthew met Robert Peary. He was an explorer. Peary visited the store to sell animal furs. The furs were from the Arctic, or the area around the North Pole. Peary asked Matthew to join his **expeditions**. Matthew said yes. They sailed to Nicaragua in Central America.

Robert Peary around 1909

In 1891, Peary and Matthew traveled to Greenland in the Arctic. They made a map of the Arctic.

In 1893, they returned to Greenland. They wanted to be the first people to reach the North Pole. Together they prepared for a long journey. Sled dogs and strong, heavy sleds called **sledges** would carry their equipment and food.

They set off on their journey. But the weather was bad. Their supplies almost ran out and they had to turn back.

Members of Peary's expedition

Peary and Matthew explored the Arctic ice cap many times over the next 18 years. It was often dangerous because of the freezing temperatures and other bad weather.

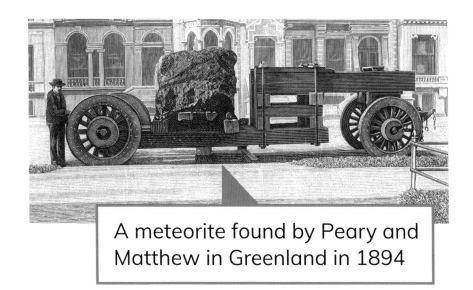

A meteorite found by Peary and Matthew in Greenland in 1894

They sailed to Greenland in 1896 and 1897 to collect **meteorites**. These are rocks from outer space. They found them on their earlier trips. Peary sold them to a museum. They needed the money for traveling.

In 1902, they tried to reach the North Pole again. They ran out of food and did not reach it.

Matthew Henson (far right)
and shipmates around 1906

They tried again in 1905. Melting ice blocked their way. In 1908, Peary and Matthew took their last trip to try to reach the North Pole. They knew they were too old to try again.

They landed at Ellesmere Island. It is off the coast of Greenland. Matthew built sledges to carry their food and supplies. He trained the sled dogs. They hired local **Inuits** to help them on the trip.

Peary with the trained sled dogs in 1907

The expedition had 24 men, 19 sledges, and 133 dogs. The long trip to the North Pole began. Slowly their food and supplies ran out. One by one, the other men turned back. Peary and Matthew pushed onward with their Inuit helpers.

The North Pole is a sheet of ice. There is no land under it. One day, the ice cracked under Matthew. He slipped into the water and almost froze to death. His Inuit helper, Ootah, rescued him.

The journey continued. The group built **igloos** for shelter. The temperature fell to minus 65 degrees Fahrenheit (minus 53 degrees Celsius). Matthew, Peary, and their team kept going. They drove the sledges 12 to 14 hours a day.

On April 6, 1909, Peary, Matthew, four Inuits, and 40 dogs reached the North Pole. Matthew put a United States flag in the ice. He had finally made it.

Family and Hobbies

In 1891, Matthew married Eva Flint. They divorced in 1897. Eva thought Matthew went away too much. In 1906, he married Lucy Ross. They were married until his death.

Matthew enjoyed visiting different countries. He liked seeing how people lived. He learned the language of the Greenlander people. They taught him how to train sled dogs and build igloos. They shared their survival skills.

An Inuit village

Amazing Explorer

Robert Peary became famous. Most people never heard of Matthew Henson. They did not know he reached the North Pole too.

Matthew worked as a clerk in New York for 30 years. He wrote a book about his polar travels. More people learned about his amazing North Pole trip. The Explorers Club made him an **honorary** member.

Matthew died on March 9, 1955. He was 88 years old. He is buried at Arlington National Cemetery in Virginia.

In 1948, Matthew holds two medals for his Arctic explorations.

Remembering Matthew

People remember Matthew Henson in many ways. He was on a U.S. postage stamp in 1986. The U.S. Navy named a ship the USNS *Henson*. Many places are named after him, including schools and a road. Matthew Henson State Park is in Maryland.

Robert E. Peary, Matthew Henson

USNS *Henson*

Matthew was a great African American explorer. He never gave up. He reached his goal. Matthew Henson stood on top of the world at the North Pole.

Important Dates

August 8, 1866	Matthew Henson is born in Maryland.
1887	Robert Peary and Matthew meet for the first time.
1891	Peary and Matthew travel to Greenland. They stay several months.
1893	Peary and Matthew return to Greenland.
1905	Matthew and Peary attempt to reach the North Pole but turn back because of the bad weather.
1906	Matthew marries Lucy Ross.
1908	Matthew and Peary begin their final journey to reach the North Pole.
April 6, 1909	Matthew and Peary reach the North Pole.
1912	Matthew's **autobiography** is published.
1948	The Geographic Society of Chicago gives Matthew a gold medal. He is the first African American to receive this honor.
March 9, 1955	Matthew dies in New York City.

Fast Facts

Name:
Matthew Henson

Role:
explorer

Life dates:
August 8, 1866 to March 9, 1955

Key accomplishments:
Matthew Henson was an important American explorer. He **charted** the Arctic polar cap. He was one of the first people to reach the North Pole.

Glossary

autobiography (aw-tuh-by-AH-gruh-fee)—a story based on the writer's own life

chart (CHART)—to make a map of a coast line

expedition (ek-spuh-DI-shuhn)—a journey to look for something

honorary (on-ur-RAIR-ee)—an honor without the usual requirements

igloo (IG-loo)—a small hut made out of snow

Inuit (IN-yoo-it)—a member of an indigenous people of northern Canada and parts of Greenland and Alaska

meteorite (mee-tee-ur-ITE)— -a rock from outer space

orphan (OR-fuhn)—somebody whose parents have died

sharecropper (SHAIR-krop-ur)—a farmer who works on a piece of land they do not own and has to share any profits with the owner of the farm

slegde (SLEJ)—a strong, heavy sled

Read More

Gardeski, Christina Mia. *All About the North and South Poles*. North Mankato, MN: Capstone Press, 2018.

Huang, Nellie. *Explorers: Amazing Tales of the World's Greatest Adventurers*. New York, NY: DK Publishing, 2019.

Jones-Radgowski, Jehan. Booker T. Washington. North Mankato, MN: Capstone Press, 2020.

Internet Sites

Matthew A. Henson Facts
biography.yourdictionary.com/matthew-a-henson

Matthew Hensen Reachers the North Pole
online.kidsdiscover.com/unit/explorers/topic/matthew-henson-reaches-the-north-pole

The Legacy of Arctic Explorer Matthew Henson
www.nationalgeographic.com/adventure/adventure-blog/2014/02/28/the-legacy-of-arctic-explorer-matthew-henson/

Index